The Little Pilgrim

The Little Pilgrim

Original edition published in Portuguese
under the title *O Pequeno Peregrino*
by Mundo Cristão, São Paulo, Brazil.

Copyright © 2009 Paulo Debs
All rights reserved.

Copyright © 2010 by Christian Art Kids,
an imprint of Christian Art Publishers,
PO Box 1599, Vereeniging, 1930, RSA

1025 N Lombard Road, Lombard, IL, 60148, USA

First edition 2010

Printed in China

ISBN 978-1-77036-359-5

10 11 12 13 14 15 16 17 18 19 – 10 9 8 7 6 5 4 3 2 1

The Little Pilgrim

TRANSLATED BY
Susana Klassen

Paulo Debs

christian art kids

IT WAS A BEAUTIFUL SUMMER MORNING when Christian received an unexpected visit. A messenger pigeon brought a very special invitation: a feast at the Palace of Lights, in the distant Kingdom of Golden Walls, in the Glorious Mountains.

Like any other child, Christian was surprised at the invitation to participate in a feast with the king. Besides, according to the letter, only a few guests would be *chosen* by the powerful ruler.

Although the boy was not really sure what "chosen" meant, he did not think twice. After putting a few things in his small backpack, he grabbed the letter and said goodbye to his parents. The trip would be long and Christian had no idea what awaited him. But he was determined not to let anything keep him from attending the feast.

IN ORDER TO GET TO THE RAVINES of the Glorious Mountains, Christian would have to walk a long way. First, he would have to cross the mysterious Woods of Dreams. Although the forest seemed pleasant and safe, many travelers had lost their way in it. Others had given up because of all traps hidden along the way.

Christian had heard many stories about the Woods of Dreams.

"I can't give up now. If I really want to go to the feast, I need to keep walking," thought the boy as he tried to muster up the courage. His legs, however, were still shaky, and even the slight rustle of leaves startled him.

AS HE WALKED THROUGH A VERY NARROW PATH, Christian came across the most cunning and dangerous inhabitant of the woods.

"Where do you think you're going, shorty?"

"Who are you?" Christian replied with suspicion.

"I'm Lord Smartfox. And you must be one of those travelers who think they can get to the Kingdom of the Golden Walls. Give up, kid! Stick around. Let's hang out in my den. The things I can teach you are much more fascinating and useful than this foolish journey of yours."

Christian was sure of what he wanted and turned down the fox's offer.

Furious, Lord Smartfox threatened:

"Move along, then, silly boy! But don't say I didn't warn you!"

AFTER ALMOST tumbling down a steep hill, Christian came to a clearing in the woods. In the middle of the green field, there was an old tree. It looked like the ideal spot to sit and eat his sandwich.

While Christian ate, he felt some drops falling on him. It could not be raining, since the sun was shining bright in the cloudless sky. Then, Christian heard someone sobbing, and wondered:

"If I'm all alone, then who's crying?"

"I'm sorry," said the big old tree. "It's me. I didn't mean to bother you."

Quite surprised, Christian asked:

"Why are you sad, Great Tree?"

"Every day Lumberjack Beaver comes by and threatens to turn me into firewood to heat up his house. He has no idea how important I am in these woods ..."

"Don't worry, Great Tree! I'll explain everything to him," said Christian while he hugged the thick trunk. "I promise I'll help you!"

A FEW MINUTES LATER, the restless and insensitive beaver came along, carrying a huge axe, determined to cut down the tree.

As he had promised, Christian placed himself in front of the Great Tree, trying to protect her from the beaver.

"Get out of the way, kid, or you'll get hurt!" warned the angry animal.

"Calm down, Mr. Beaver," said Christian. "If everybody goes around knocking down all the trees, one day they will no longer exist, because there will be no more seeds! The wind and the birds spread the seeds around. Look at these woods. Aren't they beautiful?"

The beaver pondered for a moment, scratched his chin, and somewhat embarrassed said:

"Wow! You are right. We do need trees. I will leave Great Tree alone."

So, Lumberjack Beaver went away, dragging his huge axe behind him, and thinking about what the boy had said.

Great Tree was so thankful that she let the wind blow some of her leaves to show Christian which way to go.

AS HE FOLLOWED THE LEAVES, Christian found an interesting-looking house. It seemed like a nice place to spend the night. The house looked small and modest on the outside, but there were many secrets hidden in it.

Christian knocked on the door several times, but no one answered.

Curious, the boy tried to look through one of the windows and was startled by the screech of a crow, announcing that a child was trying to escape.

Then a sinister voice coming from the house made Christian's skin break into goose bumps:

"Come back, you little runaway! Are you tired of Madame Consumer's toys?"

FROM HIS HIDING PLACE, Christian saw a strange and clever woman. She bewitched several children with things she took out of a magical chest. From the top of the fireplace, the attentive crow watched the young hostages like a sentinel.

Quietly, Christian opened the window and whispered to the boy who had tried to escape:

"Hey, you! I'll help you get out of here!"

While the woman continued to entertain the children, Christian used his slingshot to knock down the crow. The boys tried to convince the other kids to escape, but all they wanted to do was to play with the toys that came out of the magical chest.

Once they were out of the house and away from the strange woman, the two boys said goodbye to each other and went their separate ways.

From afar, he waved to Christian and said:

"Good luck, my friend! Thanks for getting me out of there!"

THE LITTLE PILGRIM decided to spend the night outdoors. He leaned his head on a rock and fell asleep. In the morning, Christian woke up feeling like there was an earthquake.

"Hey, what's the matter with this weird rock?!" the wide-eyed boy exclaimed.

"Why, of course I am not a rock, you ignorant little creature! I am a wise and renowned turtle. Besides, I am over a thousand years old. My name is Herr Whur Olde!"

"I'm really sorry! I was so tired last night that I thought your shell was a rock."

"How did you get lost around here? You aren't one of those crazy folks looking for the so-called golden kingdom, are you?" asked the turtle in a jesting tone.

"Who said I'm lost? Yes, I'm on my way to the golden kingdom. I've been invited to a feast there!"

"Oh, you silly little creature! That does not mean a thing. If this kingdom really existed, wouldn't a wise creature like me have been invited to the feast?"

"Well, I believe the seal on the letter is real. I'm sure the king will keep his word and let me into his palace."

THE TURTLE WAS NOT CONVINCED by Christian's arguments and became even more upset.

"Listen to me, boy. You will waste your time chasing this crazy dream of yours. Why don't you stay here and learn from me about the wonders of the world? I can teach you about science, history, astronomy ..." Herr Whur Olde proposed.

"I can see you're very intelligent and you've seen a lot in your long life, but to participate in the royal feast is a great honor to me, which I wouldn't exchange for anything."

When he realized that the boy would not change his mind, Herr Whur Olde retreated into his shell and pretended to ignore him.

As Christian set out, he could still hear the old turtle grumbling:

"Good luck, little creature! I hope your faith leads you in peace to the golden kingdom."

Christian resumed his journey even more certain that he would find his way to the palace.

AFTER WALKING MANY MILES, Christian finally saw the Glorious Mountains, their image reflected on the calm waters of Lake Hope.

By the shore of the lake there was a small boat with golden oars. Those who managed to get that far used the boat to cross the lake, and reach the Kingdom of Golden Walls.

Before Christian got on the boat, he noticed a slight ripple on the surface of the water, as if something were waiting for whoever dared to venture to the other side.

Christian did something smart. He picked up a few small and round stones, and put them in his pocket. He kept his slingshot at hand.

Looking around attentively, Christian started to cross the lake. The beauty of the place was breathtaking. His heart thumped in his chest. He was getting closer and closer to the Palace of Lights, where he would meet the king.

But Lake Hope had a terrible surprise in store for the little pilgrim.

SUDDENLY, WHEN CHRISTIAN was right in the middle of the lake, a huge monster came out of the water and, with a fierce roar, attacked the little boat. It was Thorment, the Terrible, a powerful and cruel crocodile that lived in the Horrid Grottos. Everyone was afraid of him. Thorment had been a prisoner in the Cave of Anguish for a very long time. Now he was free and delighted in spreading terror and agony throughout the lake.

Christian held on as tight as he could, trying to protect himself from the attacks of the monstrous reptile. The helpless boy was thrown around violently, and the impact of Thorment's powerful tail almost made the tiny boat sink.

"This is *my* lake," — shouted the crocodile — "and whoever wants to cross it has to face *me*!"

Determined to cross the lake, Christian managed to get one of the stones that had fallen from his pocket. While Thorment backed up and prepared to use its enormous tail to destroy the little boat, Christian had enough time to focus and aim at the head of the reptile.

The stone hit Thorment right on his forehead and the crocodile sank to the bottom of the lake.

AFTER HIS VICTORY AGAINST THE MONSTER, Christian reached the other shore of the lake. From there he was able to see the Palace of Lights on the top of the mountain. Not even the steep path that winded up to the palace discouraged the little pilgrim. He was determined to see the king.

A little further ahead, Christian found a traveler among the rocks, calling for help. He was very hurt, probably because of the fight with Thorment.

"It's okay, friend! I'll help you."

Although he was really tired, Christian helped the other boy climb the mountain.

"I knew this journey was a bad idea. All this trouble just for a feast!" complained the wounded traveler.

"Don't say that! This invitation is an honor to us!" said Christian, trying to cheer up his weary companion.

"What kind of honor demands so much effort from people?" grumbled once again the unhappy pilgrim.

And so, with difficulty, they arrived at the top of the mountain, right in front of the beautiful gate of the Palace of Lights.

AFTER THE BOYS KNOCKED ON THE DOOR, the servants of the palace let them in to a place where they would prepare to meet the king.

Before they were led into the banquet hall, the boys had to stand in front of the Mirror of Truth. Only those who had been chosen by the king were able to see their reflection in the mirror. Christian and the other traveler were surprised with what they saw (and with what they *did not* see!).

"But I was invited too!" argued the desolate traveler. "How come I can't see my reflection in the mirror?"

"The letter said that only a few would be chosen, remember? You haven't always been faithful to the king, and that is why you were not chosen," said one of the servants.

Following the king's orders, the servants led the weeping traveler out of the Palace of Lights and closed the doors.

Then they presented the little pilgrim with new clothes, and took him to the banquet hall, where he would meet the king.

28

CHRISTIAN SAW A HUGE TABLE covered with all kinds of delicious dishes and refreshing drinks. Everything was perfectly arranged.

Other guests entered the banquet hall through different doors and in a few minutes the place was full of people.

When all the chosen guests were gathered, the sound of trumpets announced the arrival of the king.

"Welcome, everyone! You are all my guests, and this Kingdom receives you with great joy. Let the feast begin!" the king ordered, smiling to the little pilgrim.

THAT MORNING, Christian woke up with his heart bursting with joy. Although his adventure had been just a dream, he was happy he had kept his word and been faithful to the king until the end.